Sofia-
Merry Christm
our spirited granddaughter!
We love you bunches!
        Christmas-2012
    Grandma + Papa
        Baker

Silly Frilly Grandma Tillie

Written by Laurie A. Jacobs

Illustrated by Anne Jewett

Flash
Light
PRESS

In memory of my beloved
Grandma Ida and Grandma Celia –LJ

To the ladies of the Oviedo Garden Club,
the best grandmas anywhere –AJ

Printed in China.
First Edition – March 2012
Library of Congress Control Number: 2011922642

ISBN 978-0-9799746-8-7

Editor: Shari Dash Greenspan
Graphic Design: The Virtual Paintbrush

This book was typeset in Zephyr and Gypsy Switch.
The illustrations were drawn with pencil on paper, scanned,
and painted digitally with Corel Painter to imitate the artist's
traditional painting technique of gouache, colored pencil, and salt.

Distributed by Independent Publishers Group

Flashlight Press
527 Empire Blvd.
Brooklyn, NY 11225
www.FlashlightPress.com

Grandma Tillie **says** she is too old to play games. She **says** all she likes to do is sit and knit.

But Chloe and I love when Grandma Tillie babysits because after Mommy and Daddy leave, Grandma Tillie disappears.

"I'll just sit in here and knit," Grandma Tillie says. She opens the closet door, turns on the light, and steps inside. "Sophie, you keep an eye on Chloe."

The closet door closes.

Chloe climbs onto my lap.

Then the closet door swings open.

"Hello, hello, hello!" sings the lady
with the bright pink hair.
"It's time for...

...The Tillie Vanilly Show!"

Tillie Vanilly can recite the alphabet
backwards while balancing on one leg.
She can hang a spoon from her nose.
And she can juggle and tell jokes
at the same time.

"Come on, juggle with me, girls!" says Tillie Vanilly.

"Now tell me, if food comes from farms, who grows turkey sandwiches? It's...
the farmer in the deli!"

"That's a good one, Tillie Vanilly!" I say.

"Here's another," Tillie Vanilly continues. "If a puppy leaves paw prints in a house, what kind of marks does it leave in a castle?
Paw princes and princesses!"

"More jokes, please, Tillie Vanilly!" Chloe says.

"Last one. What game did the hamburger and the French fry play? It wasn't catch, it was…"

"**Ketchup!**" we shout.

"Hooray!" cheers Tillie Vanilly. "Now, let's do the conga!"

We go "conga, conga, con-ga!"
all around the house
and into the kitchen.

"This is the end of our conga line," Tillie Vanilly says, bowing low.

Chloe and I applaud. "Bye, Tillie Vanilly! Thanks for the show!"

Tillie Vanilly walks backward out the kitchen door.

I help Chloe onto her seat.

Then the kitchen door swings open.

"Howdy!" calls the lady with the lampshade hat. "Welcome to Chef Silly Tillie's Diner. Our special this evening is worm chili with glue gravy."

"Eeeewwww!"

"Would you prefer roasted snake toes?"

"Gross!"

Chef Silly Tillie frowns. "Hmmmmm.
I don't suppose you ladies would like the last item on our menu?
It's a plain old grilled-cheese-and-potato-chip sandwich with a side of
pickles and cold chocolate milk."

"Hooray!" Chloe and I shout.

Chef Silly Tillie sings while she cooks.

"Oy my darlin', oy my darlin', oy my darlin' Clementine.
You forgot to do the shoppin', so no dinner, Clementine."

Chef Silly Tillie rolls her eyes when Chloe and I dip our pickles in the chocolate milk, but she cheers when we have a contest to see who can blow the biggest bubbles.

"I have to go potty," Chloe says.

"I'll take you," I tell her. "Bye, Chef Silly Tillie. Thanks for dinner!"

I take Chloe to the bathroom. When she's finished, I help her wash her hands.

Then the bathroom door swings open.

"Daaaahlings,"

drawls the lady with the sparkly eyeglasses and the towel turban. "I'm Madame Frilly Tillie and I'm here to make you two ladies **gooooorgeous**!"

Madame Frilly Tillie fills the bathtub with bubbles, and Chloe and I climb in.

"Maybe you should try a new look," she tells me.

She gives me a bubble beard. **"Verrry dignified."**

She puts a tower of bubbles on Chloe's head. **"Verrry chic."**

Madame Frilly Tillie
puts some bubbles
on her own face.

"Verrry gooooorgeous!"

Chloe and I laugh so hard
the bubbles fly.

Madame Frilly Tillie soaps us up and washes us down.

When we are all dry, she pats us with a fluffy puff of sweet-smelling powder.

"**Stunning**!" she says when we are dressed in our pajamas. "**Superb**! Sophie and Chloe, you two will be the most beautiful sleepers in the house. Now, off to bed!"

"Bye, Madame Frilly Tillie. Thanks for the bath!"

"I wonder who is going to tuck us in," I say. "Hiker Hilly Tillie? Or Skier Chilly Tillie? Or maybe Zoo-lady Gorilly Tillie?"

"I want my plain Grandma Tillie!" Chloe says.

Just then, the bedroom door swings
open and in walks…
            Grandma Tillie.

"You're not going to be silly now,
are you, Grandma Tillie?" Chloe asks.

Grandma Tillie smiles. "Silly? Me?
Never! I'll just sit here and read you
a nice quiet story."

Chloe is asleep before the end.

"And they lived happily ever after," Grandma Tillie says. She kisses me and turns out the light.

"Are you going to dance more?" I ask.

Grandma Tillie laughs. "Who, me? Dance? No, no dancing. Just knitting. Good night, my stunning, superb, and gorgeous little Sophie."

But as I close my eyes, I'm sure I hear my Silly Frilly Grandma Tillie dancing down the hall.

"Conga, conga, con-ga!"